Jam for Hap and Pam

Written and Illustrated by
Mary Geiger

EDUCATORS PUBLISHING SERVICE
Cambridge and Toronto

The Alphabet Series was compiled by Frances Bloom,
author of *Recipe for Reading*.

Book 1	Oops! I See a Cat!	features c, d, g, m, l, h, t, o, and a
Book 2	Tom at the Dam	reviews c, d, g, m, l, h, t, o, and a
Book 3	Tim the Hog	features i
Book 4	Jim and Cal	features j
Book 5	Kim and Her Hat	features k
Book 6	Jam for Hap and Pam	features p
Book 7	Chip Had a Hut	features ch
Book 8	Gum for a Pup	features u
Book 9	A Big Job	features b
Book 10	A Hot Rod in a Rut	features r
Book 11	A Fin in the Fog	features f and n
Book 12	Get Up, Meg!	features e
Book 13	Fun in the Sun	features s
Book 14	Tish the Fish	features sh and (hard) th
Book 15	A Wish for a Yak	features w, wh, y, and v
Book 16	Did Max Quit?	features x, z, (soft) th, and qu
Book 17	Yipyap, Too	features compound words
Book 18	My Day (by Meg)	features the ff-ll-ss-zz doubling rule

Design: Karen Swyers
Acquisitions/Editor: Bonnie Lass
Managing Editor: Sheila Neylon

Printed in Benton Harbor, MI, in June 2024
ISBN 978-0-8388-5555-3

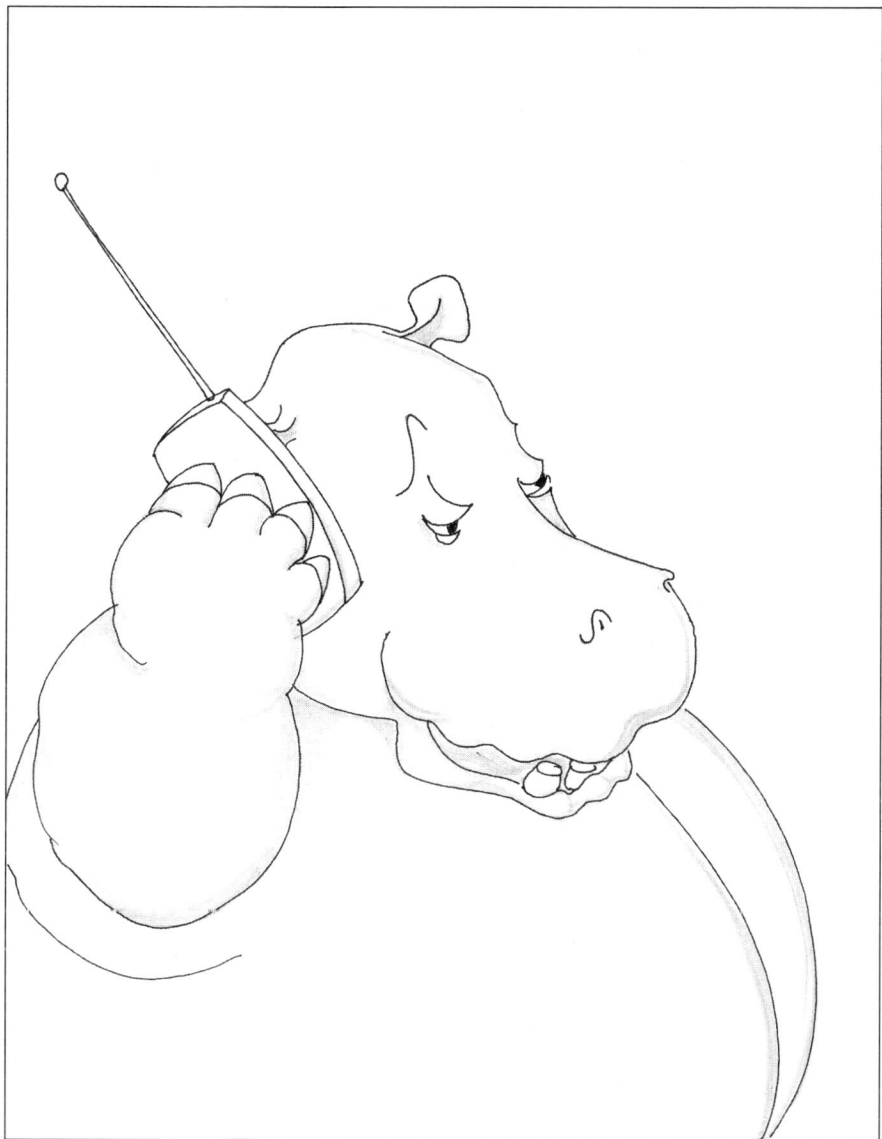

Hap had a pal.

His pal is Pam.

Pam got a pot and a lid.
She had jam for Hap.

Hap had a dip at the dam.

Hap got a cap.
The cap had a pom-pom.

Hap is tip-top!

He had to go!

Hap had to jog and jog.

He got to the tip of a pit.

Hap got on a log.

He did it!

Pam had a pot of jam
and a lot of pop.

She had a pot of jam,
a lot of pop,
and no Hap.

Tap, tap, tap.

It is Hap!

Hap and Pam had pop and jam.

What if you were having a party?
What would you do to get ready?
How would you feel if your guests
were late?

Book 6 introduces
p as in **pal**

◆▼◆▼◆▼◆▼◆▼◆▼◆▼◆▼◆▼◆▼◆▼◆▼◆▼◆▼◆▼◆

Learn ▼

he
she
to

Review ▼

a
the
and
is
on
for
go
no
of
his

Read ▼

Hap is tip-top
Pam got a pot
She had a lot of jam
a lot of pop and no Hap
he had to go